NINJA WARRIORS

by Jody Jensen Shaffer

Published by The Child's World®
1980 Lookout Drive • Mankato, MN 56003-1705
800-599-READ • www.childsworld.com

ACKNOWLEDGMENTS
The Child's World®: Mary Berendes, Publishing Director
Red Line Editorial: Editorial direction
The Design Lab: Design
Amnet: Production
Content Consultant: Dr Stephen Turnbull, Visiting Professor
of Japanese Studies, Akita International University, Japan
Design elements: iStockphoto
Photographs ©: Katsushika Hokusai, cover; Kanō Tan'yū, 4, 30
(top); Yusuke Nakanishi/Aflo/Corbis, 6, 16, 21, 23, 30 (bottom);
iStockphoto, 9; Jerry Arcieri/Corbis, 11; Shutterstock Images, 13,
18, 30 (middle); Thinkstock, 19, 24, 29; Taiso Yoshitoshi/Library of
Congress, 26; Utagawa Hiroshige, 27

ISBN 9781631437571
LCCN 2014945430

Printed in the United States of America
Mankato, MN
November, 2014
PA02246

ABOUT THE AUTHOR

Jody Jensen Shaffer is the author of 19 books of fiction and nonfiction for children. She regularly publishes poetry, stories, and articles in top children's magazines. When she is not writing, Jody copyedits and proofreads for children's publishers. She works from her Missouri home, which she shares with her husband and two children.

TABLE OF CONTENTS

Ieyasu Tokugawa was an important **shogun** in Japan.

CHAPTER ONE

THE NINJA MIND

The ninja Hanzo Hattori was pulled underwater. His general, Ieyasu Tokugawa, held him down. Hattori did not struggle. He stayed calm. He held his breath. Finally, Tokugawa let go of Hattori, swam to the surface, and gasped for air. After what seemed like a long time, Hattori came up for air, too.

The general was amazed. He asked Hattori how long he could hold his breath underwater. Hattori told him it could be as long as one or two days.

Hattori dove underwater again. Hours passed. The general started to worry. He called out for the ninja. Finally, Hattori surfaced. He was smiling and carrying the general's sword.

Ninja hid from sight to spy on enemies.

The general was shocked. He asked how Hattori got his sword. The ninja replied that after he dove into the water, he swam to shore. The ninja took a nap behind a rock until the general called him. Then he dove back in. The ninja was sorry for taking the general's sword. But he told him that it was *ninjutsu*.

This story about a ninja is a myth. But it illustrates a key principle about ninja warriors. A ninja must use brains and **stealth**, not weapons, to fool his enemies. This is *ninjutsu*, the art of stealth.

SHADOW WARRIORS

Ninja were ancient Japan's shadow warriors. They often worked for **samurai warlords**. Ninja spied on enemies during night missions. They learned to use the stars to navigate. They also studied cats' eyes to know the time of day. Larger pupils meant it was later at night.

ANOTHER VIEW
FEMALE NINJA

Not all ninja were male. *Kunoichi* were female ninja. They received the same training as male ninja. But some believe *kunoichi* were more dangerous. Female ninja did not have to sneak around at night. They posed as maids or cooks to spy on enemies anytime. Do you think it would have been harder to be a female ninja? Why or why not?

CHAPTER TWO

HISTORY OF THE NINJA

The ninja profession was passed down within families. Training could began when children were eight years old. Ninja sometimes came from farming backgrounds. When they were not spying, ninja raised crops. This gave them a good cover for their secret work. Who would guess a farmer was a spy?

Historians disagree about when and where Japan's ninja first developed. But all sources agree on one thing: these warriors were secret spies and masters of disguise. Though modern history portrays ninja as primarily **assassins**, they were much more. Their job was to spy on enemies and **infiltrate** their camps. Their goal was to get information about their enemies'

Ninja were both warriors and spies.

plans and then disrupt those plans. The word *ninja* perfectly describes what they did. *Nin* means "to endure or hide." *Ja* means "a person." A ninja was a person who endured or hid.

Because ninja operated secretly, their practices were not written down. Instead, ninja passed them to other ninja by word of mouth. What we know today about ninja was written after they were active. The *Bansenshukai* is a book of ninja methods and weapons. It was compiled in 1676 AD.

Some people believe *ninjutsu* began in the sixth century BC. During this time, Sun Tzu was a Chinese general and philosopher. He wrote the book *The Art of War*, which is still read today. Sun Tzu believed spies and disguises were important warfare tactics. The Japanese learned of Sun Tzu's teachings in the eighth century AD.

Warriors of the Iga and Koga areas of Japan were using unusual battle methods by the 11th century AD. Those areas had many mountains

JAPAN
Koga
Iga

The Art of War is still in print and sold around the world.

with lots of trees. Warriors hid in the rough **terrain** and **ambushed** enemies.

Ninja became active in Japan around 1467. At that time, Japan was divided into many different territories. These territories did not have one main government. Civil war broke out. The Onin War lasted from 1467 to 1477.

Samurai warlords fought one another. The samurai believed in a code of honor. They had rules about fighting. Samurai fought in the open. They announced their attacks with loud cries. They had many weapons and sometimes rode horses.

Going to war with other territories required different fighting skills. Warlords needed spies who moved quickly in the shadows of night. They needed smart spies to blend in with enemies and bring back information. For those times, the warlords used ninja.

The time of fighting among warlords was called the *Sengoku* period, which means "warring states." But in 1603, Ieyasu Tokugawa brought the territories together. He became the *shogun*. Ninja were not needed once peace was restored. Some were hired by Tokugawa to be his secret police. Others went back to farming or other jobs.

Samurai had very different fighting styles from ninja.

Not a Martial Art

Ninjutsu is not a martial art. In martial arts, such as judo or karate, one gains skills in self-defense and attack. Ninja sometimes used the combat skills of the samurai, such as sword fighting. But their main purpose was spying and secretly joining the enemy by using disguises.

Another View
Secondary Sources

The best source of information comes from those who experienced an event. Those people can most accurately record the details of the event. They provide primary source information. Much of what we know about ancient ninja warriors was written after they were active. The information comes from secondary sources. What are the benefits and drawbacks of using secondary sources?

CHAPTER THREE

CLOTHING AND WEAPONS

Books and movies often show ninja wearing black clothes and masks. But real ninja wore navy-colored clothes. Navy was better. The outline of black clothes could be seen in the moonlight. Ninja did not want to attract attention. During day missions, ninja dressed like regular Japanese people. They wore the clothing of farmers, priests, and monks. Sometimes they dressed as travelers or entertainers. Sometimes they even wore the clothes of enemy soldiers.

Ninja wore two-toed socks and sandals on their feet. They wore belts to hold the tools they needed. A bamboo tube kept gunpowder dry. A small box held herbs and poisons. Some ninja carried a slate pencil for

Ninja wore dark clothing and used swords.

taking notes or leaving signs on rocks. They might have also carried a rope with a hook on one end. To scale a wall, a ninja threw the hooked end of the rope over the wall. The hook caught and the ninja climbed up the rope.

Ninja used the power of surprise to outwit their enemies. Fighting was a last resort, but ninja sometimes used weapons. The weapons they carried were light, portable, and easily hidden. Bamboo blowpipes were filled with poisoned darts. The pipes looked like flutes or canes.

Ninja also used short swords. These swords were less than 12 inches (30 cm) long. They could easily be hidden in a ninja's clothes. Ninja who dressed as **Buddhist** monks carried these swords in their sleeves.

Ninja also used weapons called *shuriken. Shuriken* means "behind-hand knife." Today these are known as throwing stars. These small blades could be hidden in one's hand and thrown quickly.

Ninja sometimes used fire tools to distract enemies. They shot arrows with gunpowder-filled tubes.

THE KUSARI-GAMA

One of the favorite weapons of ninja was the *kusari-gama*. It could easily be disguised as a farm tool. The *kusari-gama* was a sickle with a chain attached. A sickle was a common farm tool used to harvest crops and cut grass. The chain on the *kusari-gama* could easily be removed from the sickle. Like a ninja pretending to be a farmer, the *kusari-gama* could also seem harmless.

Ninja also filled clay balls with gunpowder. An attached fuse made the balls explode. The smoke gave the ninja a chance to flee without being seen.

Ninja were also skilled at using plants and mixing chemicals. They learned about the area's plants and what they could do. Ninja could make poisons from plants and herbs to hurt enemies. They could mix powders that made people sleep.

A throwing star is a small but deadly weapon.

ANOTHER VIEW

UP AND OVER

Ninja used climbing tools to get into castles and enemies' homes. Rope and bamboo ladders were useful. Ninja also used hand claws and foot spikes. They used opening tools to enter buildings. Trowels could cut through doors and walls. Most of the ninja's work was done at night or in shadows. Defending a castle meant placing soldiers throughout it. But even soldiers needed sleep. How difficult or easy do you think it was for a ninja to get into a castle?

Ninja scaled walls to secretly enter enemy cities.

CHAPTER FOUR

BATTLE TACTICS

Ninja battle tactics focused on skills that one ninja could perform quietly and quickly. The goal of the ninja was to get information about the enemy. Then the ninja could find the enemy's weakness. A ninja had to sneak into enemy territory. He had to get the information he needed. Then he had to get out alive, preferably without fighting.

Ninja knew the terrain where they lived and how to hide within it. When they went into an enemy's territory, ninja first learned information about the terrain. They asked travelers and townspeople about the landscape and roads. Then they learned about enemy troops. Ninja studied their enemy's habits

Ninja learned about their enemies before attacking them.

and customs. Disguised, they lived in the enemy's community and watched.

Once inside enemy territory, ninja could remain still and out of sight for hours or days. They often hid in cramped, awkward positions and places. They put up with heat and cold without making a sound. Ninja could control their breathing and slow their heartbeats. They could go for days without food or water. They made small hunger pills from ginseng, rice, flour, and potato, to give them energy. Ninja lived off the land and used what was available to them.

Ninja had to have good control of their bodies. They moved quickly. They learned to walk silently through leaves. They crept down hallways by sliding along walls. Ninja might wear a disguise and walk with a limp to mimic an old person. Ninja could also leap high, with or without another ninja's help. They could move their joints out of socket to squeeze into and escape from small spaces.

Ninja had tactics to help them when enemies got close. A ninja might crow like a rooster or make a cricket sound to distract searchers. The searchers would then look where they heard the sound, while the ninja safely

A Ninja's Size

Ninja were not big and muscular. They had to be strong but lean. Too much weight could put them in danger. Ninja might spy from a perch on someone's roof or attic. They might crawl under the floorboards of a house. They needed to move soundlessly through water or leaves. These activities required a fast, **agile** person. Some believe ninja could lift 130 pounds (60 kg). That was what a typical ninja weighed.

Ninja climbed walls and scaled roofs to stay hidden from others.

hid. If chased by enemies, ninja threw dirt or rocks at their faces. These things blinded their enemies for a while and allowed the ninja to escape.

ANOTHER VIEW
SAMURAI VS. NINJA BATTLE TACTICS

There was a big difference between samurai and ninja battle tactics. Samurai were visible and vocal. They used many weapons. Ninja were invisible and quiet. They knew the same methods as samurai. But ninja worked at night or in disguise. Do you think it was more difficult to be a samurai or a ninja? Why?

Samurai Warrior

CHAPTER FIVE

A FAMOUS NINJA BATTLE

One of the most famous ninja battles took place in 1579. Warlord Nobunaga Oda sent his son, Nobuo Oda, to take over the Iga and Koga areas of Japan. Ninja lived and trained there. Nobuo Oda took over Maruyama Castle. He wanted to make it strong for battle. But ninja dressed as construction workers overheard Nobuo Oda's plans. They burned down the castle.

Nobuo Oda was embarrassed about the attack. He decided to attack the Iga area directly. He took close to 12,000 samurai warriors over mountain passes and into the village of Iseji. There, about 5,000 ninja attacked Nobuo Oda's forces. Some charged from the front. Others cut off Nobuo Oda's retreat routes from behind.

Nobunaga Oda fights another warrior.

The battle took place in the Iga area of Japan.

Iga ninja used guns and bows and arrows on
Nobuo Oda's forces. Fog and rain moved in. Nobuo
Oda's samurai were confused. Some accidentally killed

one another. Some killed themselves rather than be taken prisoner. Many were killed by Iga ninja.

Nobuo Oda's samurai warriors had better weapons than the ninja. But the ninja beat them anyway.

Japan's ancient ninja warriors were experts in unusual warfare. And all their work was done alone and in the shadows.

Secret Passwords

Sometimes in ancient Japan, ninja groups believed a spy was in their midst. The spy would secretly follow the ninja home after a ninja group's night attack. To prevent a spy from trying to blend into a group, ninja commanders created passwords for their ninja groups. When a ninja returned from a night attack, he would say the password at his camp's gate. But the enemy spy had no way to know this password. The enemy spy would then be revealed.

ANOTHER VIEW
CASTLE SIEGES

A ninja played many roles, such as spy, killer, and scout. But one of the most important roles was a castle attacker. While larger forces waited outside to attack, ninja snuck inside a castle, distracted the guards, and set fire to the building. When the castle guards left their posts to address these problems, the larger army could rush inside. How do you think castle guards felt about ninja attacks?

It was not easy for guards to protect castles from ninja attacks.

TIMELINE

Sixth century
BC

Chinese military writer Sun Tzu writes *The Art of War*.

Eighth century
AD

Sun Tzu's writings become known in Japan.

11th century

The people of the Iga and Koga areas of Japan become known for using unusual fighting methods.

1467

The Onin War begins. This civil war leads to years of conflict. It ends in 1477.

1467

Around this time, ninja begin working in Japan.

1467-1603

This is the *Sengoku* period. At this time, ninja are most active.

1603

Ieyasu Tokugawa unites the warring territories and becomes *shogun*. Ninja are used less and less in warfare.

GLOSSARY

agile (AJ-il) To be agile is to move quickly and easily. Agile ninja scaled walls to attack enemies.

ambushed (AM-bushd) To be ambushed is to be attacked by surprise. At night, ninja ambushed castles.

assassins (uh-SASS-inz) Assassins are murderers of important or famous people. By spying on enemies, ninja became expert assassins.

Buddhist (BOO-dist) A Buddhist is someone who practices the religion that is based on the teachings of Buddha. Ninja sometimes disguised themselves as Buddhist monks.

infiltrate (IN-fil-trate) To infiltrate is to secretly join the enemy's side to get information or do harm. Ninja frequently had to infiltrate an enemy's territory.

samurai (SAM-oo-rye) A samurai was a Japanese warrior who lived in medieval times. Samurai used loud war cries in battle.

shogun (SHOW-gen) A shogun was a military governor of Japan. Ieyasu Tokugawa was an important shogun.

stealth (STELTH) Moving in a quiet and secret way is using stealth. *Ninjutsu* is the art of stealth.

terrain (tuh-RAYN) Terrain means the ground or land of an area. The terrain in the Iga and Koga areas contained mountains.

warlords (WOR-lords) Warlords are supreme military leaders. Samurai warlords sometimes employed ninja.

TO LEARN MORE

BOOKS

Malam, John. *You Wouldn't Want to Be a Ninja Warrior! A Secret Job That's Your Destiny.* New York: Franklin Watts, 2011.

McDaniel, Sean. *Ninja.* Minneapolis, MN: Bellwether Media, 2012.

WEB SITES

Visit our Web site for links about ninja warriors:

childsworld.com/links

Note to Parents, Teachers, and Librarians: We routinely verify our Web links to make sure they are safe and active sites. So encourage your readers to check them out!

INDEX